ELEPHANT & MOUSE
CELEBRATE
HALLOWEEN

by
Lois G. Grambling

Illustrated by Deborah Maze

BARRON'S

New York • London • Toronto • Sydney

For my favorite little Trick-or-Treaters—
Lara and Tyler

All inquiries should be addressed to:
Barron's Educational Series, Inc.
250 Wireless Boulevard
Hauppauge, NY 11788

International Standard Book No. 0-8120-6186-1 (hardcover)
0-8120-4761-3 (paperback)

Library of Congress Catalog Card No. 91-15334

Library of Congress Cataloging-in-Publication Data

Grambling, Lois G.
     Elephant & mouse celebrate Halloween /
by Lois G. Grambling : illustrated by Deborah Maze.
          p.   cm.
     Summary: Elephant loves dressing up and trick-or-
treating on Halloween, but Mouse is scared.
     ISBN 0-8120-6186-1 (hardcover). — ISBN 0-8120-4761-3
(paperback)
     [1. Halloween—Fiction.   2. Fear—Fiction.
  3. Friendship—Fiction.   4. Mice—Fiction.
  5. Elephants—Fiction.]   I. Maze, Deborah, ill.
II. Title.   III. Title: Elephant and mouse celebrate
Halloween.
PZ7.G7655Ej   1991
[E]—dc20   91-15334
                                    CIP
                                      AC

PRINTED IN HONG KONG

1234   9927   98765432

Elephant liked Halloween. Mouse didn't.
Elephant liked to go Trick-or-Treating
on Halloween. Mouse didn't.
Elephant liked bumping into ghosts
and goblins and witches and black
cats in the dark on Halloween.
Mouse didn't.

The very thought of bumping into ghosts and
goblins and witches and black cats in the dark
on Halloween terrified Mouse and made
his little mouse tail quiver and shiver.
I wish I weren't such a Scaredy-Mouse,
he thought.
But I am.

Elephant went to his closet.
He took out his Halloween costume.
It was a glowing skeleton costume.
Elephant put it on and zipped it up.
"There now," he said,
"Elephant-the-Glowing-Skelephant
is ready for Halloween!"

Elephant turned to his friend.
"What will you be dressed as for
Halloween, Mouse?" he asked.
"A mouse," said Mouse.
"But you *are* a mouse, Mouse!"
said Elephant.
"Good," said Mouse.
"Then I won't have to dress up."
"But you can't go Trick-or-Treating
on Halloween if you aren't dressed
up, Mouse!" said Elephant.
"Good," said Mouse.
"Then I can't go
Trick-or-Treating
on Halloween."

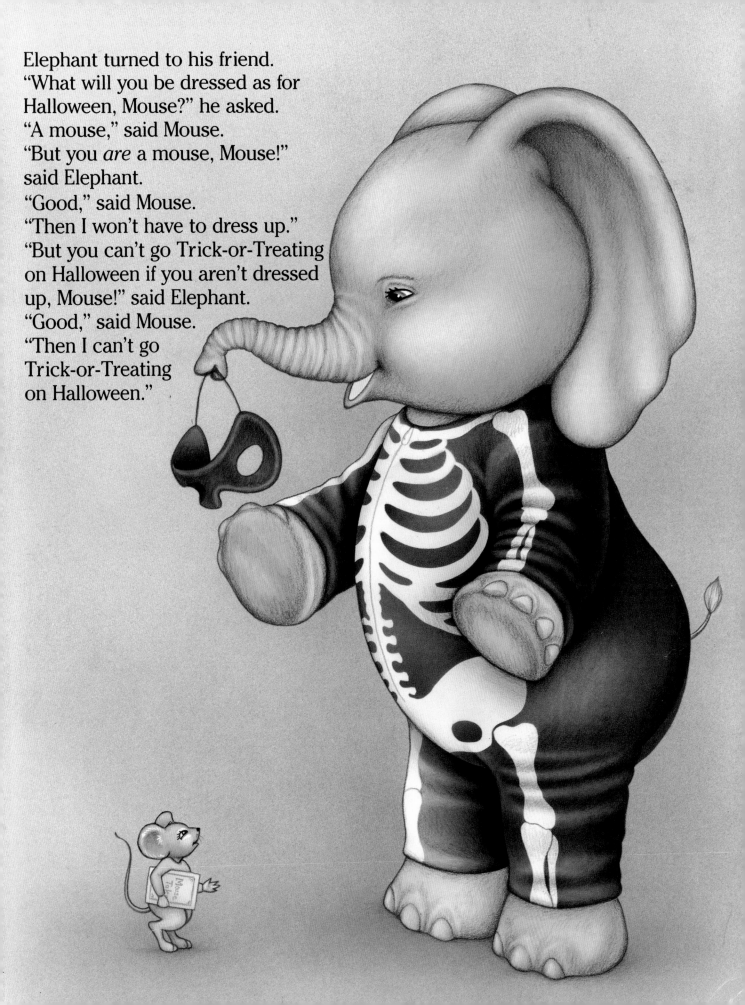

"But everyone goes Trick-or-Treating on Halloween," said Elephant. "We are friends, and I thought we would go out together." "I'm sorry, Elephant," said Mouse, "but I feel safer Halloween night inside here with the lights on than outside there in the dark." Elephant looked out the window. It was dark out there.

"But what will you do all alone
in the house tonight, Mouse?"
Elephant asked his friend.
"Sit in our big chair and hope
the doorbell doesn't ring!" said Mouse.
Elephant sighed. "Well, Mouse," he said,
"would you mind if I went out
Trick-or-Treating for a little
while without you?"
"I wouldn't mind," said Mouse.

But that was not true.
Mouse *would* mind.
Mouse would mind a lot.
But he didn't say anything to his friend.
He didn't want to spoil his friend's
Halloween fun.

"I'll be home early, Mouse," said Elephant
going out the front door. "And then we can
share my bag of Halloween treats."
"That will be nice," said Mouse,
climbing into their big chair.
The front door closed.
And Mouse was alone.

Mouse looked at the clock on the wall.
He wished Halloween was over!
But it wasn't.
He wished Elephant was with him!
But he wasn't.
He wished he wasn't such a Scaredy-Mouse!
But he was.
He wished the doorbell wouldn't ring!
But it did!
Brrrng! Brrrng!

The doorbell rang again.
Brrrng! Brrrng! Brrrng!
Shouts of "Trick-or-Treat" came
from the other side of the door.
Shadowy figures stared at Mouse
through the living room window.
Ghosts and goblins and witches
and black cats…of course!

Mouse jumped out of their big chair,
ran into their bedroom, slammed the door,
and disappeared under his bed.
Only the tip of his quivering,
shivering
little mouse tail
could be seen.

Usually Elephant had a good time
Trick-or-Treating on Halloween.
But not this year.
He was worried about Mouse.
"I shouldn't have left Mouse alone tonight,"
he said. "He might get frightened if the
doorbell rings. He probably *will* get
frightened if the doorbell rings.
IT'S HALLOWEEN!
THE DOORBELL *WILL* RING!!"
Elephant closed his nearly empty
Trick-or-Treat bag and
hurried home.

When Elephant got home,
Mouse was not sitting in
their big chair.

Mouse was not in
their kitchen.

Mouse was not in
their bathroom.

Elephant hurried
into their bedroom.

The tip of a little mouse tail was
sticking out from under Mouse's bed.
It was quivering and shivering.
Elephant got down on his knees
and looked under the bed.
"You can come out now, Mouse," he said.
"It's me, Elephant.
I'm home."

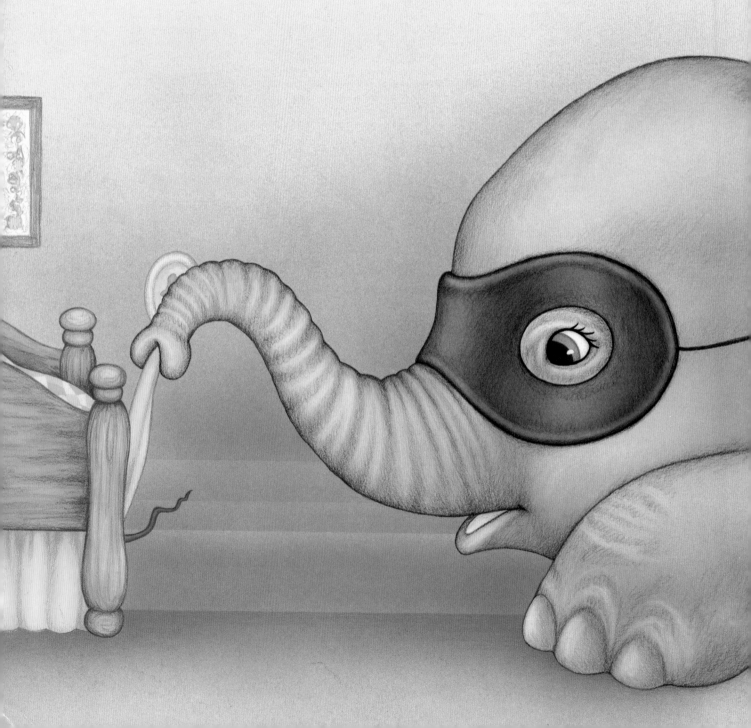

Mouse stared at the glowing Halloween
Skelephant staring at him.
"How do I know it's really you, Elephant?"
said Mouse. "You don't look like Elephant."
Elephant took off his glowing Halloween
Skelephant costume.
"See—it's really me, Mouse," he said.

Mouse's little mouse tail stopped
quivering and shivering.
"It *is* really you, Elephant!" he said.
"You came home early! I'm glad!"
"So am I," said Elephant.
Elephant helped Mouse out
from under the bed.

Elephant and Mouse sat together in their big chair.
"It's nice having you here with me on Halloween
to answer the doorbell when it rings," said Mouse.
"It's nice being here with you on Halloween to
answer the doorbell when it rings," said Elephant.
Brrrng! Brrrng! The doorbell rang.
Brrrng! Brrrng! Brrrng! The doorbell rang again.
Elephant got out of their big chair to answer it.
Mouse went with him.

"Trick-or-Treat!" shouted the four
figures standing in the doorway.
A GHOST! A GOBLIN! A WITCH!
AND A BLACK CAT!

Elephant invited them into the
living room to give them a Halloween treat.
Mouse's little mouse tail quivered and shivered.
"You don't have to be afraid, Mouse," said Elephant.
"I'm here with you now. Remember?" Mouse remembered.
His little mouse tail stopped quivering and shivering…almost.

"You don't have to be afraid, Mouse,"
Elephant said again.
"These are only neighborhood Trick-or-Treaters.
Friendly neighborhood Trick-or-Treaters.
See? They are all smiling!"
Mouse saw that was true.
Mouse smiled, too.
His little mouse tail stopped
quivering and shivering.
Elephant was glad.
So was Mouse.

"I have an idea, Mouse,"
said Elephant. "It's still Halloween.
Let's have a party. A Halloween party!"
"But who would we invite,
Elephant?" asked Mouse.
"Why, them, of course," said Elephant
pointing to the Trick-or-Treaters.
"Why, them, of course!"
said Mouse.

"Us!" said the surprised Trick-or-Treaters.
"Us!? We haven't been invited to a Halloween
party…(they put their heads together and
counted)…in over a hundred years!" they said.
"Well, then," said Elephant, "it's about time
you were! Right, Mouse?"
"Right, Elephant," said Mouse.

Everyone had a good time at the
Halloween party—even Mouse!
Bobbing for apples! Sipping hot cider.
Munching on cinnamon donuts. And…

telling deliciously scary ghost stories!
The Trick-or-Treater in the long white sheet
told the scariest ghost story!
Everyone quivered and shivered and felt
warm and good all over—even Mouse!
It was a wonderful party!

The four Trick-or-Treaters looked
at the clock on the wall.
"Oh, dear," they said.
"Halloween is almost over!
We must be on our way.
Quickly—
Or we'll turn into pumpkins!"

"We had a lovely time at your party. Thank you for inviting us," they said, as they hurried out the door and disappeared into the darkness. "Thank you for coming," Elephant and Mouse called after them.

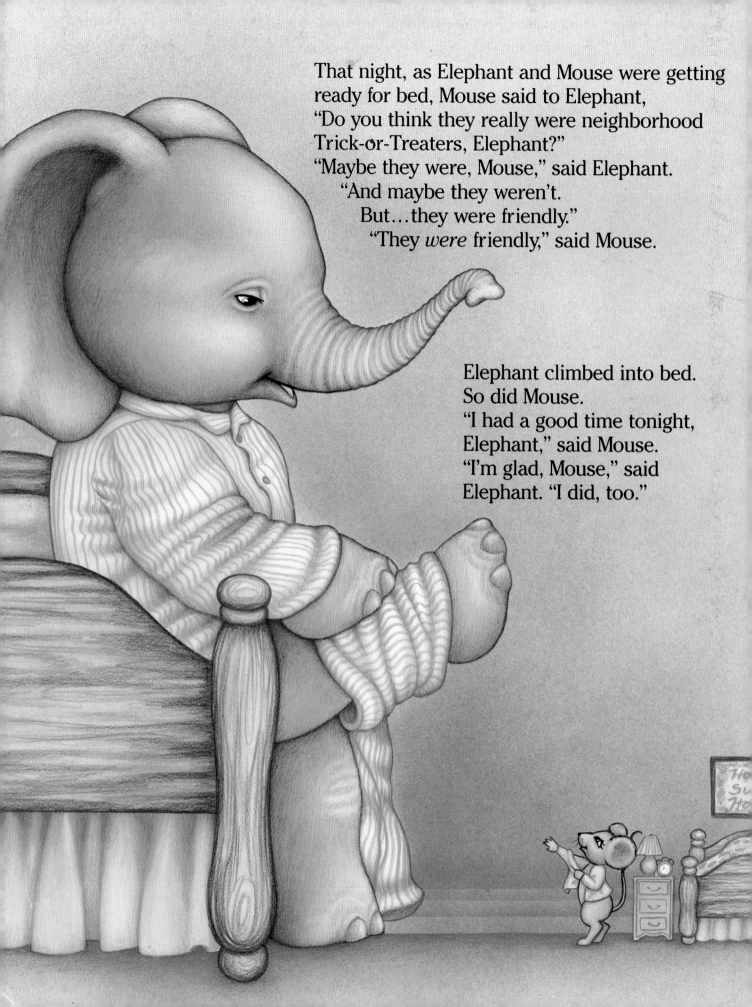

That night, as Elephant and Mouse were getting
ready for bed, Mouse said to Elephant,
"Do you think they really were neighborhood
Trick-or-Treaters, Elephant?"
"Maybe they were, Mouse," said Elephant.
"And maybe they weren't.
But…they were friendly."
"They *were* friendly," said Mouse.

Elephant climbed into bed.
So did Mouse.
"I had a good time tonight,
Elephant," said Mouse.
"I'm glad, Mouse," said
Elephant. "I did, too."

"I like Halloween," said Mouse.
"I'm glad," said Elephant. "I do, too."
"Maybe next Halloween we'll go
Trick-or-Treating together," said Mouse.
"Maybe," said Elephant. "Or maybe
we'll stay home and make
popcorn balls and candy apples—
or even have another party.
But whatever we do, Mouse,
we'll do together!"
Elephant reached over and
turned off the light.
"Good night, Mouse,"
said Elephant, smiling.
"Good night, Elephant,"
said Mouse, smiling.

And as the two friends closed their eyes
and snuggled under their blankets,
four shadowy figures, crowded together on a
broomstick, raced across the face of the big,
orange Halloween moon.

HAPPY HALLOWEEN EVERYONE!